Just Dog

Library of Congress Cataloguing-in-Publication Data available.
ISBN: 0–8118–2247-8
Distributed in Canada by Raincoast Books
8680 Cambie Street, Vancouver, British Columbia V6P 6M9
10 9 8 7 6 5 4 3 2 1
Chronicle Books
85 Second Street, San Francisco, California 94105
Web site: www.chroniclebooks.com

Just Dog

by **Hiawyn Oram**   illustrated by **Lisa Flather**

chronicle books san francisco

Dog was a dog and that's what everyone
called him. Dog. Just Dog.
   "Morning, Dog!"
   "Hello, Dog!"
   "Get down, Dog!"
   "Come on, Dog!"
   And Dog didn't like it.

He moped by the fire.

"Dog's not a name," he said to Midnight the cat. "Not a proper name. It's just something that says I'm not a cat."

"Well, you're not a cat," said Midnight.

"No," said Dog. "But I'm not just another dog either. And it's time they knew it."

Dog got to his feet, slipped out of the
back door, and began to dig up the garden.

"Have you gone crazy!" said Midnight.
"What are you doing?"

"Digging," said Dog. "Because when
I've dug more holes than any dog in
history, they'll stop calling me Dog
and start calling me Digger."

But they didn't start calling him Digger.
And they didn't stop calling him Dog.
"Bad Dog!" was all they said.
"Now what are you going to do?" asked Midnight.

WOOF
WOOF

"Bark," said Dog. "That's what I'm going to do. I'm going to bark so loud and so long, they'll stop calling me Dog and start calling me Barker."

But they didn't start calling him Barker.
And they didn't stop calling him Dog.
"Be quiet, Dog!" was all they said and they
put him on his leash.

"Now what are you going to do, Dog?"
said Midnight.

"Chew, of course," said Dog. "That's what I'm going to do. Chew through my leash and get through the fence, and chase more policemen than any dog in history. And then they'll have to stop calling me Dog and start calling me Swiftfoot, or Lionheart, or Hunter."

But they didn't start calling him
Swiftfoot, or Lionheart, or Hunter.
 And they didn't stop calling him Dog.
 "Oh Dog, oh Dog, oh Dog!" was all
they said.

"And NOW what are you going to do, Dog?" said Midnight.

"Think," said Dog. And that's when he came up with a plan.

First, he rolled over and made big "I'm sorry" eyes and gave long "I'm sorry" licks.

WHAT WOULD WE DO
WITHOUT HIM?

POSTIE'S
LITTLE HELPER

Then he tidied the
garden, was nice to the
postman, fetched all
the slippers ...

ALWAYS AT OUR
FEET

VERY TOUCHING!

didn't bark at the
neighbor's chickens,
and collected the
newspapers.

OUR NEW PAPERBOY?

He didn't run quickly through the house
but curled up quietly by the fire with a deep and
meaningful "I-am-the-best-dog-ever" sigh.
And that's when they started.
"Good Dog," they said.
"Good, good, Dog!"
"In fact, you're such a good dog, we want
to give you a good dog's name."

Sweetheart

Honeybun

Treasure Chest

"Like Sweetheart.
Or Honeybun.
Or Treasure Chest.
Or Pudding Face.
Or Sugarpops.
Or Angel Eyes…"

Pudding Face

Sugarpops

Angel Eyes

And that's when Dog couldn't help it.

He leapt to his feet, ran quickly through the house, and jumped on the sofa barking his head off!

"No, no! You've got this whole thing wrong…"

"Just Dog … SUITS ME FINE!"